Welcome to ALADDIN QUIX!

If you are looking for fast, fun-to-read stories with colorful characters, lots of kid-friendly humor, easy-to-follow action, entertaining story lines, and lively illustrations, then **ALADDIN QUIX** is for you!

But wait, there's more!

If you're also looking for stories with tables of contents; word lists; about-the-book questions; 64, 80, or 96 pages; short chapters; short paragraphs; and large fonts, then **ALADDIN QUIX** is *definitely* for you!

ALADDIN QUIX: The next step between ready to reads and longer, more challenging chapter books, for readers five to eight years old.

Read more ALADDIN QUIX books!

ROYAL SWEETS

Sugar Secrets

By Helen Perelman

Illustrated by Olivia Chin Mueller

ALADDIN QUIX

New York London Toronto Sydney New Delhi

To Lily Roth, a supersweet reader and friend
—H. P.

ALADDIN QUIX

Simon & Schuster Children's Publishing Division

1230 Avenue of the Americas, New York, New York 10020

First Aladdin QUIX paperback edition September 2018

Text copyright © 2018 by Helen Perelman

Illustrations copyright © 2018 by Olivia Chin Mueller

Also available in an Aladdin QUIX hardcover edition.

All rights reserved, including the right of reproduction in whole or in part in any form.

ALADDIN and the related marks and colophon

are trademarks of Simon & Schuster, Inc.

For information about special discounts for bulk

purchases, please contact Simon & Schuster Special Sales

at 1-866-506-1949 or business@simonandschuster.com.

The Simon & Schuster Speakers Bureau can bring authors to your live event. For more information or to book an event contact the Simon & Schuster Speakers Bureau at 1-866-248-3049 or visit our website at www.simonspeakers.com.

Cover designed by Jessica Handelman

Interior designed by Heather Palisi and Jessica Handelman

The illustrations for this book were rendered digitally.

The text of this book was set in Archer Medium.

Manufactured in the United States of America 0818 OFF

2 4 6 8 10 9 7 5 3 1

This book has been cataloged with the Library of Congress.

ISBN 978-1-4814-9481-6 (hc)

ISBN 978-1-4814-9480-9 (pbk)

ISBN 978-1-4814-9482-3 (eBook)

Cast of Characters

Lady Cherry: Teacher at Royal Fairy Academy

Princess Mini: Royal fairy princess of Candy Kingdom

Princess Lolli and Prince Scoop: Princess Mini's parents and ruling fairies of Candy Kingdom

Princess Cupcake and Prince Frosting: Princess Mini's twin cousins from Cake Kingdom

Princess Swirlie: Princess Cupcake's best friend

Princess Taffy: Princess Mini's best friend

Princess Sprinkle: Princess Mini's aunt and ruler of Cake Kingdom

Butterscotch: Princess Mini's royal unicorn

Gobo: Troll living in Sugar Valley

Lady Dot and Duke of Syrup: Princess Taffy's parents

Contents

Contents

1

Sugar Lessons

The lemon room at Royal Fairy Academy was humming with excitement. I couldn't sit still. My wings were fluttering nonstop.

Our teacher, **Lady Cherry**, was talking about Parent Night. It was

three days away. All the royal parents of first-year students were invited to school for a special night filled with candy surprises.

"Princess Mini," Lady Cherry said, looking at me. "Do you have your project ready for Parent Night?"

"I am working on it," I told her.

I sighed. I didn't know what to make for Parent Night. We had to make a candy different from our own talent. Since I am a Chocolate Fairy princess,

making mini chocolate chips is my talent and how I got my name! My mother, **Princess Lolli**, was a Candy Fairy princess and my dad, **Prince Scoop**, was an Ice Cream Fairy prince. Mini chocolate chips taste great in candy and ice cream.

What was I going to make for the ruling royalty of Candy Kingdom? Sometimes being a fairy princess was a whole lot of **pressure**.

"It is time to go," Lady Cherry said. She looked around the room. "I can't wait to see what you come

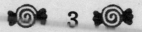

up with for your candy presenta-
tions."

"Can we work with a friend?"
Princess Cupcake asked. She
flipped her long blond hair to one
side. She smiled at Lady Cherry.
Her smile might have been sweet,
but Princess Cupcake was not all
sugar.

She was my cousin and **Prince
Frosting**'s twin. Prince Frosting
was in our class too. I knew
Princess Cupcake was not thinking of working with him. Cupcake

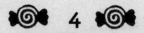

had her eye on her best friend, **Princess Swirlie**. The two of them together were sticky icky.

"I hope we don't have to work together," Prince Frosting burst out. He gave Cupcake a sour look.

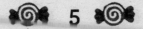

Lady Cherry took a deep breath. "Everyone should make their own candy for their parents," she said. "When your parents come to the lemon room, I want them to see something that you created by yourself."

Princess Taffy, my best friend, tapped my arm. "Did you decide what to make?" she asked.

"No," I said. "What about you?"

"Yes," Taffy said. She showed me a box of colorful candies. "My jelly beans are a little **lopsided**,

but I think they are delicious."

"I am sure your parents will love them," I told her.

Maybe Taffy could help me make taffy. She was a Taffy Fairy

from Sugar Kingdom. She had been trying all sorts of flavors lately. I was her best taster!

"Be creative!" Lady Cherry called out as we packed up for the day. "Remember, this is a chance to show your parents what you've learned in school."

The class lined up for dismissal. Everyone was talking about what they were going to do for Parent Night. I looked over at Frosting. He wasn't saying a word.

"Do you know what you will

make?" I asked. **Princess Sprinkle** was my aunt and also the ruling fairy of Cake Kingdom. She was very kind. I thought she would love anything Cupcake and Frosting made for her.

"You know Cupcake is going to do something all fancy," Frosting said. "I need to make sure mine is supersweet."

It was hard for Frosting to be twins with Cupcake, but I also knew he could be very sneaky. I was careful not to tell him

anything if I didn't want other
fairies knowing.

"What are you planning?" he
asked as he zippered up his bag.

"Not sure yet," I said.

My wings **twitched** again and I bit my lip. I wanted my parents to be proud. I knew they would expect something special from me.

Whatever candy I made, it would have to be **sugar-tacular**!

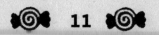

2

Gobo Treats

When the final school bell rang, Taffy and I flew out to the court-yard. I was happy I had plans with Taffy after school. She makes everything more fun.

"There's **Butterscotch**!" I said.

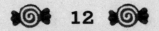

I flew over to my unicorn. She was the sweetest royal unicorn.

"Do you want to see if **Gobo** is around?" I asked Taffy.

Gobo was a tiny troll we had met near Chocolate Falls. He had surprised us and was not like the trolls we had read about in stories.

Gobo was friendly and helpful— and he wasn't interested in stealing our candy. I had helped him out of a sticky situation, and then he had helped me. We were now good friends.

 13

"Yes!" Taffy replied. "Maybe Gobo can help you with your candy project. He knows a lot about candy."

I quickly looked around to make sure that no other fairies were listening. I didn't want my cousins or anyone else finding out about Gobo. They might get him in trouble. It wasn't every day that trolls and fairies were friends.

Butterscotch stretched her big wings, and we flew up in the air. As we headed to Chocolate Woods,

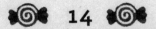

I hoped Gobo would have some ideas for me.

We landed on the soft cocoa sand by the Chocolate Falls. "I don't see Gobo," Taffy said.

"I think he is being careful," I said. "He is still nervous around Candy Fairies." I put some mini chocolate chips on the ground. "Hopefully, this will get his attention."

Sure enough, Gobo appeared. He knew the smell of my mini chocolate chips!

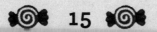

"Hello!" Gobo greeted us.

"Hi," I said.

Gobo was grinning. He held out his hand. "I found these in Sour Orchard," he said. "I thought you'd like them."

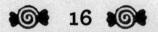

"They are so pretty," I exclaimed. A bunch of different-colored sugar cubes were in Gobo's hands.

"Sweet sugars," Taffy said. "Those look yummy."

"These would be perfect for my Parent Night project," I said.

"This is just the **ingredient** I was looking for to make my candy special."

"What is Parent Night?" Gobo asked.

"Our parents come to school and look at projects we've done," I explained. "The big project is our candy presentation."

Gobo nodded. "These candies are special," he said. "I can show you where to find them tomorrow."

"That would be **sugar-tastic**!" I said. I hugged Gobo. "Thank you!"

 18

I held up one of the sparkling cubes. "These would look delicious on a piece of caramel."

"Sure as sugar!" Taffy said.

"Meet me after school at Sour Orchard," Gobo said. "The cubes are in the Sour Caves."

I saw Taffy's face. She was panicked.

"Sour Caves?" she asked. "Sweet swirls, that place is super spooky."

I grabbed her hand. "Oh, it will be **choc-o-rific**!" I said.

"Did you pay attention to Lady Cherry's lesson on Sour Orchard?" Taffy asked. Her arms were crossed across her chest.

"Gobo will be with us," I said. "And that lesson was more about the history of sugar than Sour Orchard."

I had the perfect **combination** for a sweet candy parent project. Nothing sour was going to stand in my way!

3

Sour Exploring

The next day the school day dragged on and on. I kept looking at the clock above Lady Cherry's door. I wasn't paying attention to the measurement lesson. All I could think about was meeting up

with Gobo. I couldn't wait to get those sugar cubes!

I wanted to see the surprised looks on my parents' faces. They were going to be so proud of me!

Butterscotch was waiting for us

in the schoolyard. Taffy and I flew up to sit on her back, and we left Royal Fairy Academy. We didn't want anyone to know where we were going. After all, these cubes were my secret ingredient!

I looked over at Taffy.

"What's wrong?" I asked.

Taffy twirled her finger around her curly, dark hair. "I'm nervous about going to Sour Orchard," she said.

My wings started to twitch.

"I've heard stories," Taffy said.

She held on tight to Butterscotch's mane. "And not just from Lady Cherry. There might be scary creatures that live in the caves."

I thought for a minute as I looked down on Sugar Valley.

"Sometimes stories are made up," I told her.

"And sometimes stories are true," Taffy added.

Butterscotch flew toward Sour Orchard. From a distance, I could see why there were scary stories about the place. The trees were crooked and old, and there were strange-looking bushes.

As we got closer, I took a deep breath. There was a sweet smell of lemon and orange. This made

me smile. A place that smelled so sweet couldn't be all that bad.

"Let's land over there," I said to Butterscotch. We landed in a sour

sugar patch at the end of a row of trees. I pulled a sour candy off a low branch and popped it into my mouth.

"Yum," I said. "These are scrumptious!"

"You shouldn't eat those," Taffy told me. "You don't know what kind of candy that tree grows."

"Oh, you worry too much," I said. "Let's look for Gobo."

My mouth was watering from all the sour sweets. I knew Taffy was nervous, but I was on a

mission. I really wanted those colorful, sparkly sugar cubes.

"Gobo didn't tell us where to meet him," Taffy said. She looked around. She was still pulling at her hair. "I don't like this orchard."

"**Oh, Taffy!** Don't get your wings all low," I told her. "Gobo will be here any minute."

A cool breeze made the branches above us sway. I shivered.

Then I heard a noise. . . .

A loud crunching sound came from behind a bush.

Taffy's eyes were wide. She stood very still and waited.

I looked around. I didn't call out Gobo's name because all at once I saw who was lurking behind the bush.

Frosting! He had followed us to Sour Orchard!

4

Super Sour

"Frosting," I said. "What are you doing here?"

"What are *you* doing here?" he asked.

"Maybe I should tell your mom you have been spying on me."

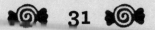

Frosting put his hands on his hips. "Just tell me what you are up to," he said.

I sighed. "I am here to get something special for my Parent Night project," I said.

Better to start with the truth, but not the *whole* truth! Since I didn't see Gobo, I thought it best not to mention our troll friend.

"Wow," Frosting said. "That is a super-sweet idea."

I held out my hand. "I thought I would use these sugar cubes," I

said. "I need to collect some more."

Frosting kicked some sour sugar sand with his shoe. "Do you think that I could use some of those cubes too?"

He asked so nicely and sweetly. I didn't know what to say.

"Come on, Mini," he said. "You know that Cupcake is going to whip up something gooey sweet. I need something special. I don't want to disappoint my mom."

At that moment, I felt sorry for Frosting. As mean as he could be, I couldn't be mean to him.

"These sugar cubes are from the Sour Caves," I told him. "I guess we can both use them."

"Thanks, Mini!" Frosting said, smiling.

"The only thing is," I said. "I

don't know exactly where the cubes are growing." I paused. "How about I bring you some tomorrow?"

"Where did you get those?" Frosting asked, pointing at my hand.

I looked over at Taffy. "Um, a friend gave these to me," I said.

"I learned a lot about the Sour Caves last week," Frosting said. "I got a book from the library about Sour Orchard after Lady Cherry's lesson."

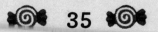

"Oh, great," Taffy said. She glared at me.

"Let's go!" Frosting said. "I have three mint glow sticks to help us see in the dark cave." He handed the sticks to Taffy and me. Then he flew straight into the Sour Caves.

Taffy pulled at my arm. "We can't go there without Gobo," she said. **"We'll get lost!** The caves are a giant **maze**!"

"Maybe Gobo will catch up with us," I said.

"Not with Frosting around,"
Taffy replied. We flew into the
dark cave after Frosting.

"Over here!" Frosting called.

"Sweet sugars!" I exclaimed.
"Look at all these sugar cubes!"

"Take a couple, and let's go," Taffy

said. "It's cold and wet in here."

My wings twitched. I opened up my bag and picked a bunch of the sugar cubes. Taffy being nervous made me nervous!

"What is that down there?"

Frosting asked. He flew deeper into the cave.

"Oh, no," Taffy said. "Come on, Frosting."

"Just a little bit farther," I said to Taffy. "These sugar cubes are **sugar-tastic**!"

"I think we should go left down there," Frosting said. He stood tall. "I do have a very good sense of direction."

"A direction aimed for trouble," Taffy muttered.

"Oh, look at these!" I exclaimed. I

picked up a handful of sugar cubes. The colors were **extraordinary**!

"There are more over there," Frosting said, flying deeper into the cave.

Taffy stood still. **"Let's go**, Frosting," she called. "I think we need to get back."

"Don't be such a worry flutter," he said. "These are extra-sweet candies, and we need them for our candy project."

I wondered if Gobo was nearby. I wished that I could see him. I

would feel better knowing he was around. I picked up a few more sugar cubes for my project. The gems were perfect!

5

Sugar Clues

"My mom is going to be royally proud," Frosting said. He tapped his bag. "This is going to make Cupcake so jealous."

"Can we leave now?" Taffy said. She rubbed her arms to keep warm.

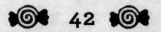

"I think you have enough."

Frosting shrugged. "Sure," he said. He buckled his bag and started to fly down the path to the right.

"Wait," I called. "I think that is the wrong way."

 43

"No, this is the way out," he said.

There were so many twists and turns in the dark caves. I spun around. "Everything looks the same," I said. "I'm not sure which way to go."

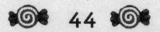

"I know the way," Frosting said. **"Trust me!"**

Taffy rolled her eyes. "I don't trust him," she whispered to me.

We flew behind Frosting. Our mint sticks were losing light quickly. I kept thinking about Gobo. Did he know we were here? Was he hiding from Frosting?

"This doesn't feel right," I said. I landed and looked around at the different paths.

Finally, Taffy had enough. "You have no idea how to get back,"

Taffy said to Frosting. "Oh, why did we follow you? What happens if we can't get out?"

"The opening to the cave should be around here," he said. "Don't get your wings all tied up yet."

"The mint sticks are losing light," Taffy said. "You know there are licorice bats and other sour gummy creatures in here."

"Stop," Frosting said. His lip **quivered**. His eyes were wide as he looked around the cave.

"Are you afraid?" Taffy asked.

"No," Frosting said, a little too fast.

"Look out!" I cried.

A licorice bat flew across our path.

Taffy screamed.

I ducked.

Frosting's eyes bugged out.

He burst into tears.

"Maybe this wasn't a good idea," he whispered.

I stared at him. The prince of cool, Prince Frosting, was afraid of licorice bats!

"The bat is gone," I said. "He wouldn't have hurt you."

Frosting rubbed his eyes dry. "You don't know that," he said. "Those bats are slick and sour."

"Wait, look!" I said.

 48

Sure enough, I saw a sign that Gobo was there. Who else would have set a line of sugar cubes?

"Follow me," I said.

"This could be a trap!" Frosting cried. "There might be more bats that way."

At that moment, I knew Taffy and I had to let Frosting know about our secret friend. I looked Frosting in the eye.

"You need to make me a promise," I told him. "I need to

know you can keep a secret."

"Sure," Frosting said.

Taffy shook her head. "Don't say anything," she said to me. **"I don't trust him."**

"Taffy, our wings are up against the wall," I said. "We have to tell him."

Frosting looked hurt. "You can trust me," he said. "Really."

"If you tell anyone," I warned, "I will tell the whole school you are afraid of licorice bats and

cried when you saw one."

Frosting turned. "You wouldn't," he said. "That would be super sour of you."

"I won't say anything," I promised, "if you don't say anything."

"What are you both talking about?" Frosting asked. **"What is this big secret?"**

"It's *who* is this big secret," Taffy said. "And you have to promise, Frosting."

Frosting took his finger and

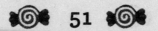

made an X across his chest. "I
promise," he said.

"Gobo!" I called. "It's safe.
You can come out."

I watched Frosting's face as
Gobo appeared from behind a
rock.

"Frosting, this is our friend Gobo," I said.

For the first time ever, Frosting was speechless.

6

Sweet Secrets

"Does your friend speak?" Gobo asked.

Frosting was just staring at Gobo.

"Usually, he can't stop talking," I said.

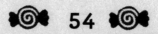

"Is that a . . . tr-tr-troll?"

Frosting finally asked.

"Yup," Gobo said. "And are you a prince?"

I pushed Frosting forward. "Gobo, this is Prince Frosting, my cousin," I said. "He is from Cake Kingdom. You can trust him."

"I don't trust him," Taffy said.

I gave Taffy a cool stare. "We have to trust him," I whispered. "And there is no way he wants that bat secret getting around Royal Fairy Academy."

 55

Taffy looked over at Frosting. "This secret better be caramel sealed," she said. "Gobo doesn't need to worry about you blabbing around school."

"I will not say a word," Frosting said. "But will he really get us out of here?"

"Yes," Gobo said, grinning. **"Come this way!"**

We followed Gobo down and around the small, dark path. Finally we made it to the opening of the cave.

"This is the coolest secret I have ever had," Frosting said.

I sighed. "Gobo is a special friend," I told him. "I think that you will think so too."

Gobo bowed and smiled. "I have never met a prince before," he said.

"And I have never met a troll, so I guess we're even," Frosting replied.

"This is going to work out," I said, smiling.

Taffy crossed her fingers. "I

hope so," she whispered.

"You can count on me," Frosting said.

Parent Night was super fun. It was strange to see the lemon room so crowded with grown-ups. All the parents were very happy to see the work we had done. **And there was a ton of special candy!**

Lady Cherry rang her bell. "Welcome to the lemon room," she said. "Please feel free to

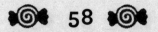

taste all the candy and ask the students about their work."

Across the room, I saw Frosting. His candy looked sparkly and delicious, too. I winked at him. It felt good to know that we had a sweet secret.

Cupcake was showing her mother her fancy gummy flower with sugar crystals. Swirlie made a licorice flower. Their candy was supersweet, but Frosting's was truly **sugar-tastic**.

I could tell Cupcake was not

prepared for Frosting's chocolate bark with sugar cubes to be
so good. She was in full sugar
mode, trying to keep her mom's
attention.

Frosting waved to me. I could
tell he was feeling very proud.

I showed my mom and dad to my candy.

"Where did you find these sugar cubes?" my dad asked. He held up a piece of my candy and smiled.

"Oh, you should know not to ask a Candy Fairy her secrets," I said, grinning.

"Wow," my dad said. "These are delicious." He licked his fingers. "You chose caramel candy. A hard candy to make."

"And difficult to decorate," my

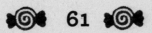

mom added. She held the candy in her hand. "The sugar cubes are scrumptious and colorful." She gave me a tight squeeze. "I am so proud of you, Mini."

I felt my face get very red like a licorice twist.

"Thanks, Mom," I said.

Taffy's parents, **Lady Dot** and **Duke of Syrup**, gave her jelly beans a great review.

Taffy waved me and Frosting to the back of the room. "Did you see Cupcake's face?" she asked. "Frosting, you really surprised her."

"I know," he said. He grinned widely. "My mom said the sugar cubes were icing on the cake!"

 63

"We pulled off the **assignment**," I said to Frosting and Taffy.

"Just remember your promise," Taffy warned.

Frosting nodded. "I will. Don't worry."

I was glad Frosting was now part of our secret friendship. He might be sour at times, but he had proved to be a loyal friend. I knew that our secret was safe. We had many more adventures in store for us!

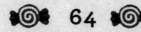

Word List

assignment (a·SINE·ment): A task that must be done

combination (com·bi·NAY·shun): Two or more things put together

extraordinary (ek·STROR·di·nair·y): Far beyond the ordinary

ingredient (in·GREE·dee·ent): An item used to make a recipe

lopsided (lop·SI·ded): Uneven or not perfect

maze (MAIZE): Confusing set of pathways

mission (MI·shun): Important job or task

pressure (PRE·shur): Stress

quivered (KWI·verd): Moved with a slight shaking motion

twitched (TWITCHED): Moved quickly and suddenly

Questions

1. Why does Princess Mini feel pressure about her Parent Night project?

2. Why is Taffy nervous to go to Sour Orchard?

3. Where are the sugar cubes found?

4. How do Mini and her friends get out of the cave?

5. What candy would you make for Parent Night?

CHUCKLE YOUR WAY THROUGH THESE EASY-TO-READ ILLUSTRATED CHAPTER BOOKS!

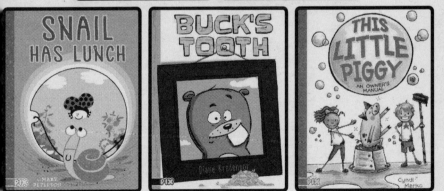